Part 4 of the Summer Series

Amy Sparling

Copyright © 2015 Amy Sparling
All rights reserved.

This book is a work of fiction. Names, characters, places, and incidents either are products of the author's imagination or are used fictitiously. Any resemblance to actual persons, living or dead, business establishments, events, or locales is entirely coincidental.

ISBN-13: 978-1512189889
ISBN-10: 151218988X

Cover art from shutterstock.com
Cover design by Amy Sparling
First edition May 18th, 2015

Dedication

To all of my readers who started reading Bayleigh's journey and finished with Becca's. A loyal reader is an author's greatest asset.

Chapter 1

"Trick or treat!" A tiny little Batman holds out an orange plastic jack-o-lantern, his toothy grin spilling out from under his mask.

"Happy Halloween!" I say, digging into the bowl of candy and giving him a heaping handful. My boss Ollie had told me to pace myself with the candy, but I can't help it. Cute kids get lots of candy. Besides, we have like ten more massive bags of assorted Halloween candy in the stock room. Ollie probably just wants leftovers so we can gorge on them in the next few weeks.

"I like Captain America, too," the boy tells me as he steps aside so the next girl in line can get some candy. I wink at him and then smile at his parents as they shuffle him out of the door and toward the next store in the in Lawson Outdoor Mall. C&C BMX Park is located at the very end of a long strand of outdoor shopping stores, which makes up the only good shopping center in Lawson. LOM always does this big Halloween celebration, encouraging all of the stores to give out candy to kids so their parents are more likely to do some shopping as well as trick-or-treating.

I love it because we don't get many trick-or-treaters in our neighborhood so there's never any fun in handing out candy at home. Plus, now that I have the excuse of having to work, I can get out of party invites.

I know. I'm a loser. But underage house parties meant for getting wasted and hooking up with random people never really appeal to me. I used to only go when my best friend Bayleigh forced me to, but now she's married and has the cutest little kid ever, so she doesn't hit up the party scene either. I smile and hand out candy to a little girl dressed as Elsa from Frozen. She's about the hundredth little Elsa I've seen tonight.

My phone vibrates loudly from under the front counter. When my line of trick-or-treaters have fizzled out, I set down my plastic Captain America shield and find my phone, hoping for a message from Park. He's on his way to Texas from California and should be here in an hour or so, depending on traffic.

And yes, I'm dressed as a not-so-sexy Captain America. I chose the costume both because Captain America is the hottest Avenger, and because I didn't have any time to make my costume this year, thanks to freaking college midterms. Government and History are not my friends. In fact, they might just derail my college career before I've even reached my junior year.

I had spent the last week fretting over these freaking mid-terms. At home, I studied my butt off and at work, I did the bare minimum of my job requirements and then studied discreetly at the front counter until my shift was over. As much as I love my boyfriend, it's a good thing he hasn't been able to visit in a few weeks. Otherwise, my grades would have been toast.

Instead of making my own costume, I was lucky enough that I had some spare time to swing by the Halloween store after class today. It's a shame that all of the costumes for women have to be ridiculously sexy and skin-baring. I remedied that by wearing black tights under my red, white, and blue spandex booty shorts and I safety-pinned a piece of white lace between the cleavage of my sexy Captain America tank top.

The absolute last thing I'd want is to have my boob fall out while I'm handing a four-year-old some mini Snickers bars.

Disappointingly, my new text isn't from Park. It's from the other 'ark' in my phonebook—Mark. The guy I stupidly went on a date with last semester. I was in a dark place, missing companionship and feeling like Park and I would never work out. But after going on one measly date with Mark, I know I would have stayed far away from him even if Park and I never got back together.

To put it plainly, he's kind of a creeper jerk.

I sigh and open the text even though I already know the gist of what it'll say. He's been texting me randomly every week or so, asking me out on another date, or worse, asking for very filthy favors when he's been out drinking. My simple replies of No thanks don't seem to deter him. Bayleigh insists that I tell Park about it, have him answer the phone next time Mark calls and tell him to go away. But I don't want to bother Park about this. He's been busy with his motocross career and with fixing up the house he bought on my side of town.

He's acting like everything is cool and fine but I worry. It's weird now. Things have always been weird with the idea of dating someone who lives two thousand miles away and has a career and apartment on the other side of the country. But now that Park went off and bought a house in Lawson, Texas without even telling me about it first, is just another weird layer to our complicated relationship.

Buying a house seems like a super expensive way to visit your long distance girlfriend. And what does it even mean, anyway? I know he has money from racing professional motocross for a few years, but still. It's weird.

Mark's text message makes me grimace. It's not the worst one he's sent, but it's no friendly hello either.

Send me a picture of that sexy ass costume you're wearing.

My skin feels like something's crawling on it as I look up, half expecting to see him and his drunken friends standing outside of the BMX park, watching me with creepy sneers. They aren't, luckily. A man with a ton of tattoos walks in with three little girls, all dressed as princesses.

I shrug off the disgusting text message long enough to give them candy and compliment their awesome handmade tiaras. The moment they leave, I look at my phone again and realize something. How does he know I'm wearing a costume? Is it just a lucky guess?

What makes you think I'm wearing a costume? I text back, even though I should probably just ignore him.

Because it'd be a crime for someone as hot as you not to dress up.

I scowl. I'm working. I don't have time for this. Please stop being gross.

A few more kids come in and my phone doesn't go off for another half hour. I'm feeling good, like maybe he finally got the message to leave me alone, or maybe he's just bothering another girl, hoping for a sleazy photo to hit his inbox.

Guys don't make any sense to me. Why would they want photos of girls when they can just get all the nakedness they want by searching for it online?

I ask Ollie this when he returns from his office, wearing a Dracula cape and plastic fang teeth. He didn't really put much effort into his costume, but that's better than nothing. The other guys who work the BMX part of the shop didn't dress up at all.

Ollie lifts an eyebrow and looks at me as if I've grown an extra head. "You kids really blur the lines between boss and friend, ya know?"

"Sorry," I say, feeling my cheeks blush. "I shouldn't ask you that. It's just annoying when guys I barely know ask me for dirty pictures. It's like why the hell do they want it?"

He laughs. "Men are idiots, Becca. But I'm proud of you for not doing things you feel uncomfortable with. If that guy keeps asking, I'll send him a picture of my hairy ass. Maybe that'll shut him up."

I laugh at the thought of sending a picture like that to Mark. That would be hilarious. More kids come in to trick-or-treat and Ollie makes his best Dracula impression, which is actually quite horrible, and then heads out to pick up dinner for us. Tonight we're getting Magic Mark's oven-toasted sandwiches, which are to freaking die for. I love having a boss who acts like friend, gives me advice like a mentor, and buys us dinner when we're at work.

Around nine p.m. the trick-or-treaters have pretty much fizzled out, but it's a Friday night and the BMX park is open until midnight. Some of the teenage riders beg me for candy, and since we have hordes of it left over, I give in and let them take an unopened bag back to the locker room. Food is strictly prohibited on the track, so I give them my meanest, most threatening glare and tell them to keep the food and the empty wrappers in the locker room.

I settle back down on the stool at the front desk, casually browsing through Pinterest on the work computer. Someone walks in and I look up with a Professional Employee smile on my face.

The smile quickly falters.

Mark strides up to the front counter, reeking of pot. His eyes are glazed and he smiles lazily at me. "Trick-or-treat," he says, widening his smile. "I didn't bring a candy bag, so maybe you can put the candy in my pockets."

I take a deep breath and let it out slowly, turning back to the computer screen. Ollie has already gone home for the night, but I could easily call one of the guys from the back on the intercom. They can kick him out if he refuses to leave on his own.

"Aw, come on," Mark says, stepping up to the counter, pressing his hands against the aluminum countertop. "I'm just playing. I don't need any candy. I just came for some eye candy." He bursts into laughter and I swear he could do a perfect impression of Beavis and Butthead with that stupid, stoned laugh of his. "Do you get it?" he says. "Eye candy?"

Of course I do, but I want to put him on the spot. Make him feel as uncomfortable as he makes me feel. "No." I fold my arms across my chest. "Explain it to me."

He leans forward on his elbows and I take a step backward from the counter. His eyes drift to my chest. "What I mean, is there's two pieces of candy for my eyes right in front of me. Since you wouldn't send me a picture, I had to come see them for myself."

I look him straight in the eyes. "You're gross."

The doors slide open and I ready my candy bowl for the incoming children. It sucks that I have to step away from the protective wall of the front counter to give out candy, but with any luck, if I spend a long time putting candy in kid's bags, maybe Mark will leave.

He seizes his opportunity and grabs my arm, almost making me drop the candy bowl. A short and chubby pirate runs up to me, holding out his pillowcase full of candy.

"Trick-or-treat!" he squeals, but his little voice can't drown out the words Mark says while he's gripping my arm. "Aw come on, Becca. You didn't think I was gross when you went out with me."

My jaw sets so tightly it makes my neck hurt. I twist away from him and try to focus on the little kid in front of me. Someone appears on the other side and then cuts in front of the kid just as I'm about to drop candy into his pillowcase. The candy spills everywhere and when I look up, confused, I see what caused me to be shoved backward.

"Hi there," Park says to Mark with a smile that could level mountains. "Get your fucking hand off my girlfriend."

Chapter 2

Mom and Dad are asleep when I get home just after midnight. Park leaves his truck on the side of the road instead of pulling into the driveway, which lets me know he plans on staying a while. Dad leaves for work really early in the morning, so Park will only block in Dad's police car if he's not staying very long.

Ever since I turned nineteen, my parents got kind of cool about letting me do whatever I want. Yeah, I'm a legal adult and everything, but it's still their house, and I kind of expected that they wouldn't let Park stay over late, but they really don't care. Dad had told me once that me hanging out at home is the safest place for me to be, so of course he doesn't mind if Park is there, too. He said it's a thousand times better than the shit he has to deal with at work; murders, runaway teenagers turned drug addicts, etc. Honestly, I don't want to know what the etc. is. It's a terrifying thought.

I grab my purse, lock my car, and jog down the driveway to where my super, crazy hot boyfriend is still sitting in his truck, his face lit up by the glow of his cell phone.

I tap on the driver's side window and he rolls it down. I make this big exaggerated frown. "Why are you rolling down the window? Get out so we can go inside!"

He sets the phone down in his lap and I sneak a glance at the screen. He's looking at his emails. "I'm not ready to go inside," he says, nodding his head toward the seat next to him. "Get in."

"It's after midnight. Where are we going?"

"My new casa," he says, his eyes going wide with excitement. "I closed on it today."

He holds up his hand and I slap him a high five, then I shimmy around the front of the truck and climb inside. Hopefully Mom and Dad won't wake up, find my car and not be able to find me, and freak out. Actually…I send Mom a quick text telling her that Park and I went to get ice cream at the twenty-four hour grocery store. Hopefully she won't wake up, but if she does, she won't have to freak out and think I've been murdered.

A couple of months ago, when Park decided to drive all the way to Texas and surprise me after weeks of us not talking, he had given me a key and claimed it was my key to his new house. That was kind of true. He had been in the process of buying the house for a few weeks, and once he knew he would officially get the house, the rushed out and got the keys made just so he could make some huge romantic gesture to me before he had actually closed on it.

The house in question was a foreclosure that had been vacant for a few years, so the bank took forever to get all the paperwork and stuff finished on it. So my house key, all shiny and new, was just a symbolic gesture for the house we couldn't quite go inside of yet.

Until now.

When I had asked why he didn't just wait until the house was closed on and officially under his ownership to give me the key, he had said he couldn't wait that long and risk losing me forever. Park may be a rough around the edges, hardcore motocross guy, but the boy sure knew how to be romantic when he needed to.

Park's new house is situated on the very edge of Lawson's town border. It's near the river and in the absolute middle-of-nowhere, just a mile north of where the interstate takes you on an hour-long drive to Mixon, Texas, home of lots and lots of empty boring land and, of course, Mixon Motocross Park.

Mixon, although just a dot on the map, is close to my heart. It's where Bayleigh lives. If you speed and don't get caught, the drive is only forty-five minutes, so it's not so bad. Still, I miss her like crazy, even if she did used to make me go with her to house parties.

We pull into the driveway, which needs a new pouring of concrete because the one that's there now is all broken up an disheveled from tree roots growing underneath it. Park and I have been here a couple times, usually just sitting in the driveway looking at it and talking about all the ways the front yard could be landscaped.

Now, we get to go inside. "When did you get the power turned on?" I ask as we walk up the overgrown pathway that leads to the front door.

"Today. I had to stop by with an electrician to make sure everything was wired okay and that nothing would catch on fire or anything. That's why it took me so long to get to your work tonight." At that, a flash of a grimace crosses his face. He was not in a good mood when he walked in and found Mark hassling me. "I unplugged all of the appliances just in case. Everything passed inspection though, so that's good."

Park's new house is an older home, built to look like a Victorian, but it's not that old. It's two and a half stories with a wraparound porch that has a swing hanging near the front door. On the third floor is a peak with a big bay window that Park said would be my painting studio. It overlooks the backyard which has a small creek flowing through it that meets up with the river a few miles down. I think he only owns a few acres of land here, but the land goes on and on for miles, so the view is beautiful.

The white exterior needs repainting and the black shutters could use a fresh coat of paint as well. Park had warned me that this place was a fixer-upper, but as we walk in through the massive wooden door, I'm surprised that it's not nearly as bad as I had imagined.

Hardwood flooring groans beneath our feet as Park leads me from the foyer into the living room. It's massive and has a beautiful fireplace in the center of the biggest wall. The walls are painted baby blue and are dotted with nails from where the former resident's pictures used to hang. "We have to get rid of this ugly blue," Park says, motioning for me to follow him into the kitchen. "You might want to close your eyes," he says, placing his hand on my lower back. "And you know, just don't open them at all," he says with a snort of laughter. "The kitchen is ugly as hell."

I ignore his advice and look at the kitchen anyway. "You're right. This kitchen is balls ugly," I say, tapping my finger on the forest green Formica countertop. "But it's huge, and that's a good thing." The kitchen is open and angular, with tons of cabinets and counter space. There's an island in the middle with a bar and two French doors that open out into the back yard.

Park nods and sits at one of the leftover barstools. "Here's the plan: This bullshit linoleum is going tomorrow. I've got some guys who are going to rip it up. We're going to put eighteen inch square tiles down." He points to his finger as he lists off his renovations. "Granite countertops and brand new cabinets. These are just the worst," he says, looking with disgust toward the white painted cabinets. "And all new appliances, obviously. Fresh paint. It'll be perfect after that. Same thing with the bathrooms. They're all being totally gutted and redone. I'm not even going to show you those because they're so blah and outdated."

I smile. "Look at you. All fancy and homeowner-like. You're talking like...oh I don't know, a thirty-year-old."

He gives me his sideways smile and motions for me to come closer. I walk up to him, wrapping my arms around his neck and stepping in the space between his legs while he sits on the tall barstool. We kiss and then he lets his forehead touch mine for a moment. "I love you," he says, his breath warm on my lips.

"I love you," I say back. My fingers hold on tightly to the back of his neck. I need him close. I need him with me. I miss him so much when he's gone that sometimes I miss him when he's right here.

"I could use some help picking out appliances and stuff," he says a moment later. I stand up straight, keeping my arms around his neck. He slides his hands into the tiny back pockets of my Captain America booty shorts and now it's hard to concentrate on anything but the feel of his hands on me.

"Hmm," I say, trying to concentrate despite his distractions. "I guess I could be convinced to go appliance shopping with you. But you'll have to buy me ice cream or something because shopping for appliances is bor-ring," I say, singing the last word.

"All it takes is ice cream? Psh. Easy."

I roll my eyes at him and he pulls me in, snuggling his face against my neck and kissing me repeatedly until I squeal and pull away. "Have I told you that you look hot as hell in this costume?" he asks.

"I don't think you have," I say. He slides his hands to my hips and tightens his grip. When his eyes trail down the length of my costume, I don't get the creepy-crawly gross feeling like I did when Mark did the same thing. That's because Park is allowed to ogle me. I love when he thinks I look cute.

"Well, you look crazy hot." He wiggles his eyebrows suggestively. "I should have knocked out that asshole who couldn't keep his eyes off you."

"I know, but I'm glad you didn't. I don't need you in jail on Halloween," I say. Earlier tonight, Park had shoved Mark against the wall, blocking Mark's airflow by pressing his forearm into his neck. After some colorfully threatening words, Park had led him go, but not after telling him he has eyes all over this town and that he better not hear of Mark talking to me again.

I have to admit, it is kind of hot seeing a guy get told off by your boyfriend. But the look Park got on his face when he recalled the incident told me he didn't think it was funny, or hot.

He shows me the guest bedroom and office downstairs and then we head upstairs and check out the other two bedrooms and the master bedroom. This house could easily fit a family of six and yet, Park is just one person.

"Why'd you get a house so big?" I ask once we're finished looking at the massive closet in the master bedroom.

He shrugs. "I liked the location of this house much better than the smaller ones that are for sale. I did look at some condos in town and at a new neighborhood near C&C. But I can't stand that cookie cutter, homeowner's association crap in those neighborhoods. Plus, your neighbors would hear everything you say since those houses are so close together."

"True," I say. "This place is just so…big."

"Well I'll have a family one day to fill it all up."

The next few moments of silence are filled with heavy thoughts from both of us. I break the awkwardness by saying, "Oh, really? How are you going to pull that off?"

He shrugs and takes my hand as he walks me down the hallway and to a narrow staircase just off the main stairs. "Guess I'll have to find a girl, fall in love with her, and then convince her to marry me."

"Sounds like a good plan..." I say, feeling all wobbly and tingly in my toes. He squeezes my hand. "Looks like I've already accomplished the first two things."

My body flushes from head to toe. Thankfully, this hallway is dim thanks to a broken light fixture in the ceiling. He shows me the storage closets and built-in nooks, and takes me up the narrow staircase to the studio room at the top of the house, but as we walk around, I don't really focus on anything he shows me.

I'm too busy thinking about what he just said. What he implied. Does Park want to marry me? Could I really get this lucky? Is he thinking about proposing? Has he bought a ring? Or is he just suggesting generic ideas for the future? I'm not sure it's possible for me to get as lucky as Bayleigh did with Jace.

I'm sure he was just talking, just making up hypothetical ideas of things that he might want to do some day. I shouldn't get so worked up and let my imagination run wild.

Besides, why would he want to marry me? I'm just...me. Ugh. Just boring Becca Sosa from boring Lawson, Texas.

"Babe?" Park's voice breaks me out of my depressing thoughts. I look up and find that we've reached the top of the staircase and are standing in a little foyer that leads to a closed door. "This is where the best room in the house is. Your studio, if you wanted."

I go to step forward but he holds me back. "Sorry, we can't go in."

"What?" I say, frowning. "Why not?"

"Because it's under renovation. The people who owned this house let their stupid kids draw all over the walls and make a mess of it. I can't let you see it until it's ready."

"I'm sure I can imagine what it'll look like when it's fixed up."

"Sorry," he says, kissing me quickly on the lips. "It's a surprise."

"Fine," I say with a relenting sigh. "I'd rather spend time with you anyways. I haven't seen you in forever."

Back in Park's truck, we hang out in the driveway and I slide over the bench seat until I'm pressed up against him, my knees bent and my feet in his lap. "Wanna go back to my place and make out?" I say with a goofy grin.

His hand grabs my knee and slides down my thigh. "Absolutely, I do. But you'd have to move over so I can drive and I definitely don't want you to move." He gives me his puppy frown and I roll my eyes.

"So what's been up in the millions of years since I've seen you last? How's work?" Park doesn't have a job like most people do, in that he doesn't go to an office every day. He races motocross under a professional sponsorship team with a dozen other racers. There's usually a race every weekend during the supercross season. Park took a break from supercross this year, choosing only to race the outdoor summer season.

He shrugs and plays with my hair absentmindedly. "I love this costume on you, by the way. Have I said that yet?"

"Only like a million times." I nudge him with my shoulder. "Tell me about work. How's the dirt bike and all that jazz?"

"Oh, it's good," he says quickly. "Really good. Since, well... I just quit."

"Wait, what? How did you quit a professional contract? How do you just quit something like that?"

He shrugs. "It wasn't hard. besides, I'd been thinking about it a long time."

"But Park!" I have to force my mouth to close since all it wants to do is hang open. "Racing is your life. That's what you do. You're no one without racing. You say that all the time."

He shakes his head. "Not necessarily. I'm no one without dirt bikes. I can live without racing. Besides, I know you're like the most encouraging person ever, but I had to face the facts. I'm no champion racer. I'm a top ten person. I always will be."

"Babe, you can't be so hard on yourself," I say, knowing that it kills him when he doesn't finish in the top three."

"It's not that," he says. "Racing is tough. I had my time in the spotlight and I loved it. But it's time to move on with my life. Like Jace did. Find a real career and not just hold onto the hope that I'll win enough money to retire at the age of thirty."

"You're only twenty-two," I say. "You have a long time to get better at racing."

He shakes his head again. "I don't want to. Besides, it's done. Apparently someone still refuses to subscribe to the motocross news, because it's been all over the web, people talking about my quitting."

"Yeah well, call me crazy but I choose not to sign up for that stupid thing." After what happened last time I looked on the motocross news websites, when I found pictures of Park with some super hot girl on his arm, I decided I'm better off in the dark about the world of professional motocross.

He runs his fingers through my hair, watching me carefully. "Becca, I did what was best for me. It's not that big of a deal. Besides, now we get to spend more time together."

I smile and try to swallow the lump in my throat. I should be happy, ecstatic even, that my long-distance boyfriend just quit his job and is becoming my in-town boyfriend. But quitting the world of professional motocross isn't nearly the same thing as if I were to quit my part time gig at C&C BMX Park. In fact, it's about a million dollar contract different.

He doesn't say it but it doesn't have to. I know he's made these decisions because of me, because of us. So we could be together in a real way. It should be everything I'd ever dreamed of, but instead it feels like a nightmare.

How am I supposed to be happy that Park gave up everything for someone as boring and epically not special as me?

Chapter 3

On Monday, I'm supposed to have lunch with Bayleigh and her super adorable baby boy, Jett. But then, thanks to the hyper awareness that Monday brings a person after a weekend spent making out and picking out paint colors with your boyfriend has deluded your thoughts, I remember I have an essay due for my history class on Wednesday.

It's kind of a major grade in a class that I'm kind of close to failing, so as I much as I don't want to work on it, I know I should. So instead of taking a two hour lunch break from work and meeting up with her, I ditch her very politely and apologetically via text message.

Work is slow on Mondays during the school year; the only people coming in to ride are older guys who gave up on school years ago. No one really shows up in the morning at all, because those kinds of guys definitely don't wake up at in the morning, so I know I'll be good to study.

My phone beeps and I check it to find a pleasant surprise. My Etsy store has sold another one of my canvas paintings. Well, they're not really paintings per say. I use a canvas and I paint a quote on it, usually something inspiring or motivating. Sometimes the quotes are from famous people, other times it's anonymous. Some of my art work contains just one word—

like LOVE or LIVE or SUNSHINE. I paint the canvas and add mixed media pieces to give it dimension and depth.

It started out as a hobby based on my love of inspirational quotes, but Park encouraged me to sell my artwork on line. So far this week, my online shop has sold six canvases. Now, make that seven. I smile and get back to studying.

I'm standing behind the counter at work, pouring over my stupid college history textbook when the big glass doors slide open. In comes Bayleigh, lugging what looks like a super heavy baby carrier on one arm, Jett knocking around inside of it with every step she takes. In her other hand, she balances two Taco Bell bags, two drinks in the crook of her elbow, and her cell phone. The lanyard that holds her car keys is fitted between her teeth. She smiles at me in this crazed, over-worked mom kind of way.

I rush forward and grab the baby carrier, making goo goo faces at the baby as I relieve her of its weight, and I set it on top of the counter, right in the middle so there's no chance baby Jett will fall off.

Bayleigh looks amazing. After a few months of depression from being stuck at home all day, she had decided to do something about it. Now she fixes her hair and gets fully dressed each morning, saying it helps her feel like she has purpose. It's good to see her happy again. I know she stresses about not having an official job, but as her husband and I always tell her, taking care of the baby is a super important job.

"I know you said you're too busy to go out for lunch," she says, hoisting the Taco Bell bags onto the counter and handing me a drink from her elbow. "But you didn't say anything about staying in for lunch, so I took some liberties and brought it to you."

"Thanks," I say, opening the bags and setting out their contents on the counter. Bayleigh and I eat Taco Bell in what we call Family Style—meaning we order a crap ton of food and randomly eat parts of all of it at once. "I only brought a Pop-tart for lunch so this is kind of awesome."

Baby Jett watches us intently as we start in on our food and I feel bad that he can't have any. Bayleigh gets some melted cheese on her finger and holds it out to Jett, who eagerly licks it, only to make a sour face.

"So when are you going to spill it?" I ask, eyeing her suspiciously over my crunch taco.

"Spill what?" She bats her eyelashes at me. "Can't a girl just come hang out with her best friend without having any other motives of wanting to know all the juicy details about why her best friend's boyfriend just totally moved down here from California?"

I laugh and throw a nacho chip at her, which she catches and promptly eats. "I don't really know what to say about Park. I mean, it's exciting but it's scary, you know?"

She considers this a moment and then shakes her head. "How is it scary? It's awesome. I was psyched when Jace moved down here."

"Yeah but Jace already had ties to this state because he inherited his grandfather's house down here. Plus, he's like crazy in love with you."

"Park is crazy in love with you," she retorts. "And he has ties with you and his best friend, who happens to be my husband, who happens to live in Texas."

I take a bite of a burrito. "Still scary."

"No, what would be scary is if Park had asked you to move to California and then I'd have lost my best friend. I'm a very needy person," she says with a smile. "I can't have you moving across the country, you know."

"Don't worry, that won't happen." My phone beeps to signal a new text message. I lean over and see Park's name light up on the screen. Without reading it, I slide the phone back toward the work computer and continue eating.

Bayleigh lifts an eyebrow. "Oh my God, are you thinking of breaking up with Park?"

"What? No." My reply is quick. Too quick. Her eyes go wide and she grabs my arm. "Becca. You can't lie to me."

I shrug. "I'm not lying. I mean, I don't know."

Wow. That's the first time I've admitted it both out loud and to myself. When it comes to my relationship with Park, I really don't know. I mean, sure we had fun this past weekend but things were weird. An awkward nagging feeling tugged at me during the time we were hanging out, and I think he felt it too. It was like ever since the moment he bought that house, things have been different for us.

That doesn't mean I don't love him. I do, I just...

I glance up from my thoughts and find Bayleigh giving me a deadpan stare. "What's going on? You can tell me, you know. I won't tell Jace."

Now it's time to admit something I really haven't been allowing myself to think. I take a deep breath. "I don't think I'm worth it. He's given up so much of his life for me, to be here and to be with me, and I just can't stop feeling like it's all a huge mistake on his part. I mean...look at me."

The ten seconds of silence that follows my monologue makes my heart leap into my throat. Bayleigh isn't immediately saying anything reassuring. She's not doing her best friend duty to tell me what I want to hear. She's just...watching me. Finally, her smile contorts into something resembling pity.

"Honey, you need to talk to him."

"I will," I say. "We're just eating lunch right now so I'll text him back when we're done."

"No, I don't mean that." Funny how ever since Bayleigh became a mom, her I'm Serious And You Better Listen to Me face has become honed to Oscar-worthy perfection. "I mean you need to sit down with him and have a talk about everything. About why he moved here and your future together and all of that. If you don't think you're good enough for him, then he needs to assure you that you are."

"And what if he doesn't?" I say. "What if he can't assure me of anything?"

"He wouldn't have moved here if you weren't good enough for him."

I shake my head. "I don't know. Maybe he moved down here for another reason and I'm just his girlfriend until he figures out what he wants to do with his life."

Bayleigh grabs my half-eaten burrito and takes a huge bite. "Talk to him."

I draw in a deep breath and let it out in a sigh, bringing my forehead all the way down to rest on top of my open history book. "You're right," I say into the pages. "I'll talk to him."

Chapter 4

I don't talk to him. For three days, I manage to avoid any serious conversations with Park and stick to just basic hello, goodnight, see ya later texts. It turns out that all of my studying for the history midterm did absolutely nothing for me, because instead of facts and figures and dates, the entire midterm was a two hundred question vocabulary test. Luckily, about half of the class also failed it and our instructor is allowing a retake to make up half of the points we missed. He had said we were lucky this was only "community college" because "real college" doesn't work that way.

Seriously, screw that guy.

But now that I have a reason to lock myself up in my room for a few days and study some more, I use it to my full advantage and make it my excuse for avoiding Park.

And I hate that I'm doing this. Park. MY Park. The gorgeous, sweet, super freaking hot guy who I am currently dating and up until a few weeks ago, would have never believed that I'd avoid him like this. Things change though, and you can never underestimate the power of a guilty conscious.

Around five in the afternoon, I get a text from Park. Although I'm lying on my back on my bed, propped up by a bunch of pillows with my open notebook of vocabulary words in my lap, I've been accidently watching Netflix for the last hour.

Park: Wanna grab some dinner?

Just seeing the word dinner makes my stomach ache. I'm starving and Park loves all of the same food places that I do. Brendan always whined whenever I wanted anything other than pizza or burgers.

Me: Totally. Pick me up soon?

Park: Be there in 20

Even though I spend the next few minutes getting dressed and brushing my hair, twenty minutes blows my quicker than it feels. There's a knock at my door and I glance behind me, seeing Park's truck waiting on the side of the road. With one last look in the mirror, I frown at how my highlights are growing out pretty terribly, and then open my bedroom door.

"You don't have to knock and then wait out in the hallway, you know," I tell Park as he walks inside my room. He doesn't answer. He just slips his hands around my waist and pulls me toward him, making his lips crash into mine. As we kiss, the feel of him so close to me makes my heart ache with longing. I'm starting to think we'll never stop kissing each other until I hear Mom's footsteps on the stairs.

We pull apart and I take a few steps backward until I'm in front of my easel. Mom appears in the doorway. "Park said you were going out for dinner? Could you get me something to go?"

"Sure," I say, feeling my chest heave with the leftover adrenaline of making out with Park just seconds ago. "We don't know where we're going yet."

"That's fine, just call me when you get there and I'll pick something." She digs through her jeans pocket and takes out a twenty dollar bill.

"It's on me," Park says, waving her hand away and flashing her that million dollar smile of his. Mom smiles and gives his arm a good squeeze. "Thank you, dear. I appreciate it."

Behind his back, she gives me that little smirky smile thing that's supposed to be secret code for how much she likes my boyfriend. I roll my eyes but deep down I'm glad Mom likes Park. Because I like him too. And I should really stop avoiding him and figure out a way to make this life with him perfect and not guilt-inducing.

Now if only I can accomplish that without throwing up on myself first.

"So is anything bothering you?" Park asks before he's even taken a bite of his burger. We're at a local diner, which ended up being our last resort when we couldn't think of a better restaurant for dinner. But as it turns out, it was a great choice because the burgers are freaking delicious.

"Honestly, Park…" As soon as the words are out of my mouth I close it back up again and begin stirring the sugar around my sweet tea.

"You definitely need to finish that statement." Park sets his burger down and looks at me. "You're not about to break up with me, are you?"

"What? No!" I shake my head so furiously it might fall right off my neck. "No, babe. I love you. A lot."

"Good," he says, letting out a breath. "As long as that's clear, take your time letting me know what's wrong." There's a smile at the corner of his mouth as he takes a bite. "Damn these things are good."

"That's what I told you five minutes ago," I say with a laugh. "But no…you had to eat fries first."

He shrugs and takes another bite. "We should come here more often."

I nod. "Totally."

"So what's wrong?"

I roll my eyes. "You told me I could take my time."

"Yeah and it's been like two minutes. Surely that's enough time?" He winks at me when I give him an annoyed look.

"Fine." I take a long sip of tea and then sit back in my chair, feeling a flood of nervousness pour through my chest. I don't want to say these things but I know I need to. I can't live my life this way, constantly worrying about stuff that might be fixable. I take a deep breath. "Okay, Park. Here's what's wrong. I love you and you love me and things are great," I begin, feeling my fingertips shake with worry.

"How is that a problem?" he interjects.

"You moved here. You bought a house. You've made like a million sacrifices in the last month just to be with me."

He nods. "It's called love. What's the problem?"

"I—I just..." I close my mouth and breathe, trying to think of the right thing to say. "I worry that you're getting ahead of yourself. That you've made too many sacrifices for our relationship and that maybe it's not worth it. Maybe you'll wake up one day and realize you don't really like me that much."

Park wipes his hands on the cloth napkin and then sets it back in his lap. His fingers clasp together in front of him and he leans forward just a little bit. "That's not going to happen, Becca."

"How do you know that?"

He shrugs. "I just do."

My eyes burn with the sting of tears as I call forth the words I've been desperate to say, but haven't yet. "How do you know you want to be with me forever when we haven't even had sex yet?"

There. I did it. Quietly, so no one else could hear, but I did it.

"Becca. Is that what's bothering you?"

I nod, looking at my hands. Now even this delicious burger doesn't look appetizing.

He puts a hand on mine and squeezes it. "Honey, that's not a problem at all. We'll get there when you're ready and it'll be awesome and there's nothing to worry about."

"How do you know what? What if you hate hating sex with me? What if I'm terrible at it?"

He laughs. Actually laughs. "Honey I'm serious. That won't happen. Trust me, sex doesn't determine if a relationship is good."

"Trust you?" I blurt out loud enough to make the couple in the next booth over look back at us. My hands turn to fists and I pull away from his grasp. "Right, okay. I'm so glad I can trust you on this."

"Becca, what is wrong? Of course you can trust me."

I shake my head, feeling rage and embarrassment and all kinds of stupid emotions crash into me all at once. I stand from the booth and toss my napkin on the table. "Okay well great. I'm glad you're so freaking experienced in the subject that you can tell me without a doubt that sex won't change anything. So glad you know that."

"Becca..." Park goes to stand, but I turn away and leave. I don't want to hear what he has to say. He can't make it better. He can't change the fact that he's experienced as hell and I am so not.

Chapter 5

Bayleigh's car is in the driveway when I get home after class. She had texted me asking for a last-minute babysitter and I told her I'd be available at five. I glance at the clock on my dashboard—it is exactly four fifty-two.

Jett's laughter bursts through the front door as I make my way inside. Mom is on the floor in our living room, making gooey baby faces at him while he stands on shaky little chubby legs, playing with her.

"You're early," I say, dropping my books and purse on the coffee table. Mom excuses herself saying she has a hair appointment and threatens to steal Jett so she can show him off to her friends at the salon.

As soon as she's out of the house, the door closing securely behind her, Bayleigh's eyes bug out of her head. "I'm early because I need time to chat with you before going to the movie with Jace."

"What's up?" I ask, kicking off my shoes and settling down with Jett on the floor. He hands me a stuffed bunny that he carries with him everywhere and I make the bunny hop around until Jett laughs.

"You tell me what's up," she says, giving me those eyes that says she's up to something mischievous.

"I have no idea what you're talking about."

She folds her arms over her chest and looks at me with her creepy mother-knows-all look. "Well then tell me why Jace was on the phone with Park last night, telling him not to worry and that it'll be fine?"

"He said what?" My outburst ruins the calm composure I had tried so hard to develop. "Jace and Park talk about stuff like that? But they're men."

"Men can call up a friend to complain about relationship problems you know. So tell me what happened. Why was Jace telling him it would be fine? Did you two get into a fight?"

I shake my head. "No I'm just being impossible as always."

"He didn't say that," Bayleigh says, although I'm certain she's lying. Jace tells her everything but he's also a guy and guys don't share details because they're typically too bored to recall them.

I try to busy myself with Jett but Bayleigh is insistent. Finally, after glancing in the driveway to make sure Dad's not home and Mom's car is officially gone, I tell her. I tell her about my worries and my fears and the sex thing.

It's the sex thing that makes her mouth fall open.

"You haven't had sex yet? Like, seriously?"

Blood rushes to my face and I shake my head. "Nope."

"Have you gotten close?"

"I mean...not really."

"Wow!" Bayleigh laughs and then immediately claps her hand over her mouth. "I'm sorry. I don't mean to laugh. Look at you, you're so well adjusted and proper. That's impressive."

"It isn't funny, Bay. It's actually annoying. See, I can't stop worrying that not only is he leaving his entire life behind to come here and be with me, and that's got its own problems, but what if he does all of that and then finds out that I'm terrible in bed?"

"Everyone's terrible in bed at first," Bayleigh says. "If Jace wasn't super helpful with me then I'm not even sure I'd have known what to do," she admits. Her cheeks blush a moment later. "Besides," she says, shrugging off the memories that had so obviously formed in her mind, "Park will do the same with you. You won't totally suck at sex, I promise."

"How can you promise me that? You haven't had sex with me."

Bayleigh rolls her eyes. "I promise you that Park will like having sex with you. If he doesn't, I'll give you a money back guarantee."

We laugh and then I lie on my stomach to play with Jett as he baby crawls across the living room rug. The sex thing is still on my mind but I'm trying very hard not to let it get to me. To pretend that everything is cool and peachy and fine.

"I gotta go," Bayleigh says a few minutes later. "I didn't realize date nights were so great until I didn't have them for a few months."

"They say it keeps a relationship together," I say, dolling out advice I've only heard secondhand.

I walk Bayleigh to the door and she shakes her head. "No, honey. Date nights don't keep us together…" Her eyes narrow and she gives me this creepy look. "The sex does!" She cracks up into laugher and I shove her toward the door. "You can go away now," I say, glancing back at Jett who is starting to fall asleep with his bunny in his arms.

"Seriously though," she says, stopping in the doorway and putting her tiny hand with its massive diamond ring on my shoulder. "Don't let sex stress you out. It's supposed to be fun."

I sigh. "It's like, every day it doesn't happen is another reason for me to worry. Sex wasn't that big of a deal at first and now it's a huge deal, at least in my mind."

Her lips squish to the side of her mouth. "Park hasn't been asking you to do it?"

I shake my head. "He's too….gentlemanly."

This gets a laugh out of her and if I were in her position, I might laugh too. After all, Park had the reputation of being a ladies man before I met him. "The fact that he used to be some kind of player and now he's in a relationship with me and hasn't—you know—I just, I wonder if there's something wrong with me."

Bayleigh's eyes go serious and she squeezes my shoulder. "Don't you dare say that, Becca Sosa! You are so good enough for that boy. You're better than good enough."

"Thanks," I say with a smile that's so forced it probably looks like a frown.

"I love you," she says. "This will be okay. You'll see."

"I love you, too," I mumble back as I watch my best friend skip down my driveway without a care in the world.

Chapter 6

The next morning, my phone's vibrating wakes me up at an hour that should be off limits unless there's some kind of emergency. Wait. Maybe it is an emergency. I flop over in bed in a panic, thinking the worst. Maybe Bayleigh is calling form the emergency room of Lawson General.

But the moment my sleepy eyes focus on the cell phone screen, I frown. It wasn't a call or a text that had sent my phone into hyperactive buzzing mode—it was alerts from my email. Apparently I sold a few paintings.

Wait… no.

All of them.

I sit up in bed, tossing off the comforter because suddenly everything's gone all hot on me. This must be some kind of glitch in the system—there's no way I've sold all seventeen paintings I had listed on Etsy overnight.

Grabbing my laptop from underneath my bed where I had shoved it before falling asleep, I power it up and wait for the page to load. Sure enough, all seventeen of my listings have been purchased over the last few hours. Most of them from separate buyers, although a few people bought more than one.

I do the math in my head. At thirty five dollars each, I now have six hundred dollars in my bank account. I can't believe that so many people actually care about the art that I've created. It's one thing to see my canvases and think they're cool, but the fact that people actually spent their money on my creations brings a tear to my eye. Maybe a career in art really is viable. Maybe I really can succeed.

Even though my computer tells me it's four fifteen in the morning, I'm too hyped up with excitement to go back to sleep. Luckily, I don't have work in the morning, so who cares. I climb out of bed and drag out all of the canvases I've made in the past two weeks but have been too lazy to list online.

With my cell phone, I take pictures of them and upload them online, along with descriptions. I keep them at the same price, a modest and respectful thirty-five dollars each. Park and my mother have argued that they should be priced higher, but I just can't justify charging more for something I enjoy making.

Another thing that Mom had been talking about occurs to me as I finish the new listings. I'll need to pay taxes and stuff on my income. I'll need a separate bank account to keep businesses expenses and income organized. Maybe I'll go down to the bank in the morning and open one up, under my business name: Becca's Inspirations.

I know, I know. It's a super original and unique name. My talent lies in painting artwork, not naming it.

I sell another painting just a few minutes after I've listed fifteen more. The rush of getting another sale sends chills down my spine and has me reeling with the desire to make more paintings as soon as possible. I glance around my room and take inventory — only three blank canvases left. I should probably start finding a way to buy them cheaper than at retail.

Now it's nearly five in the morning and I'm no longer sleepy. With the adrenaline rush of thinking that my love of art could maybe, possibly, if I get lucky enough, become a career, I set up my easel and get to work on another inspirational saying.

My quote board is filled with ideas, but I don't bother consulting it because I know exactly the quote for the deep blue paint I'm smoothing over the fresh canvas.

Every day is a second chance

I make the letters tall and narrow, with little curls at the end of each one. The canvas is deep blue with swirls of lighter blue fading into the background. The words are black, but after painting them, I go over them with a watered down silvery paint to let them shine. It's gorgeous and I can't stop smiling when I sign my name to the bottom corner.

My phone buzzes again and I grab it, feeling the pitter patter of my heart getting excited about another sale. Only it isn't a sale, it's a text from Park. At six in the morning.

Luckily, I don't have time to panic and think something terrible has happened this time because his words scroll across the screen the moment I look at the phone.

Park: I love you. Even though you're blah about me.

I smile and look at the time again. Why is he up so freaking early? There's no way he's expecting a reply this soon because he knows I sleep as late as possible on my days off. So I figure he'll be excited to see my reply.

Me: I love you

I look at the screen and then quickly type a second text.

Me: And I'm not blah about you.
Park: Shit did I wake you?
Me: Nope.
Park: Ok. I love you.
Me: You already said that.
Park: Just saying it again ☐

Exhausted from waking up so early and from my spur of the moment painting, I lie back on my bed and hold the phone out so that I can see Park's picture as my wallpaper. Sometimes, during moments like this, I realize just how much I love that boy. Freaking out about our future and sex and all kinds of other things doesn't really do anything but stress me out. For now though, I am happy. I love Park and he loves me.

Without thinking, I call him. He answers on the second ring.

"Hey baby." His voice is all throaty and sleepy and it makes me miss him a thousand times more than I already did.

"Hi," I say back, sighing into the phone. "I just wanted to call and say I love you."

"I'm glad you did. What's up over there?"

"Not much," I say, staring at the ceiling with my legs hanging off the edge of the bed. "I couldn't sleep so I painted another canvas."

"I can't sleep either. I hate when things are weird between us."

I sigh. "Things aren't weird. I'm the weird one. I'm sorry."

"Don't be sorry. Hey, are you doing anything this morning?"

"No...why?" I ask.

I can hear Park shuffle around on the other end of the phone. It sounds like he's getting out of bed and walking somewhere. A door opens. "How about I come pick you up and we get some breakfast?"

"At six in the morning?"

"We could come back to my place and fall asleep after." Even through the phone I know he's giving me his alluring, ultra-hot gaze. My stomach knots up and my mouth goes dry.

"Yeah," I say, sitting up in bed and thinking of something to wear. "That sounds good. I'll see you in a few minutes."

Chapter 7

Park brings me home around noon and we practice our fabricated story about where we've been all morning in the truck. "You'll say you wanted to get to the donut place first thing in the morning so all the good donuts wouldn't be gone and I'll say after we ate, we decided to check out the farmer's market." I nod to myself as I come up with this plan while Park drives toward my house. "Mom knows the farmer's market is open early in the morning and that's where all the good produce is sold. The place is crap in the afternoon."

"Okay but there's two problems with that story," he says, drumming his fingers on the steering wheel.

"What's that?"

"One, you don't have any fruit purchases. Do you really think she'd believe that you went to the place with the best blueberries and didn't buy any?"

"True," I say as my shoulders fall. "Maybe I ate them all on the drive back?"

He shrugs. "Maybe."

"What was the second problem?" I ask. The radio starts playing some awful song that sounds like animals trying to kill each other inside of a metal barn. I reach up and turn down the radio. Park glances at me and smiles. "I don't think your parents will care that we went out early in the morning. I mean, it's better than going out late at night, right?"

I consider this a moment. "You might be right. I don't know. This is my first time doing boyfriendly things at random hours. I'm not really sure what my rules are."

"You're nineteen. The rules can't possibly be that restricting."

"True. Maybe we won't tell them anything."

Park sits straighter and smiles. "If we have kids one day, I hope they're as sweet as you. Then I wouldn't have to sit up all night with a shotgun when she goes on dates."

"That was...out of left field," I say, feeling my throat dry up. Doesn't he realize that to have kids with me means we'd have to have sex first? Maybe he wants to adopt kids. Whatever the case, he just mentioned having kids with me and now I am freaking out.

My parents don't say a thing when we get home. Score one for Park. Mom is eating a sandwich in the living room and Dad is passed out next to her on the couch. It's weird realizing that one day you're a legal adult and your parents just don't care what you do anymore.

I still haven't said anything about Park's mention of our future children, instead choosing to do the easy thing and change the subject. We head into my bedroom and I plop backwards on my bed. "I'm still tired," I say with a yawn.

Although Park and I had snuck in a few hours of sleep this morning, it hadn't helped much.

"What happened to the rest of your boxes?" Park asks. He's on the other side of my room, eyeing the corner that used to be stacked with unfolded triangle mailing boxes. What started out as a stack that came up to my hip, is now a stack only knee-high.

"They got shipped out all over the country," I reply, feeling warmth rush to my cheeks. I don't know why it's embarrassing admitting that a lot of paintings have sold. I guess I still feel weird about the idea that people want to buy my stuff.

"Damn, girl." Park joins me on the bed, lying on his stomach next to me on my back. "I told you people would love your work."

"I've almost made a thousand dollars so far," I say. As if it heard me bragging, my phone vibrates and I check it then turn the screen around for Park to see. "Look, I've sold another one."

"Thirty-five bucks? Babe you should charge a lot more. Like twice as much."

I shake my head. "I can't do that...it's weird."

He takes my hand in his and brings it to his lips. "Why is it weird?"

I shrug. "It's just weird that people are spending money on my art."

Park chuckles and kisses the top of my hand again. "Honey, your work is amazing and it's original and I hate to say I told you so, but…"

"But what?" I say, rolling my eyes.

"But I told you so," he says with a laugh. "You're going to be a famous artist one day. And I'll be that artist's boyfriend."

"I'm hardly famous. You're the famous one."

"I tell you what," Park says, leaning over and kissing my cheek. "We'll both be hardly famous together."

Later, after Park left, claiming he had something to do with Jace, the smell of Mom cooking dinner brings me out of my painting trance and into the kitchen. I had been painting a series of canvasses with romantic quotes on them, no doubt because of the massive amount of love Park had left me with, flowing through my veins and all over my heart.

I know I don't know much about love, but when your heart aches for them while they're still in the same room with you, that has to mean something. And now that he's been gone a few hours, my heart aches more than ever before. I think I'm finally ready to take our love to the next level—the sex level—but I need to make sure all of my bodily issues are gone before letting Park know this.

Mom notices my good mood the second I walk into the room. "What's up with you?" she asks, pointing a spatula at me. "Sell more paintings?"

"Yeah, actually. But that's not why I'm smiling."

I take a seat on the barstool at the kitchen island and watch as she quickly chops up hamburger meat and then moves to grating a block of cheddar cheese. Immediately, I regret the last words out of my mouth because they make my mother give me one of her Mom Looks.

"Really? Well then why are you smiling?"

I shrug. Stare at the counter. "No big reason or anything."

"Park left kind of early, didn't he? I take it you're not fighting or anything?"

I shake my head. "He had some appointment with Jace or something. Said it was boring motocross stuff. He'll be back later."

"Ah ha," Mom says, nodding to herself as if she's suddenly got everything in the whole universe figured out. "So it's something to do with Park."

"No," I say with a groan. "Can't a girl just smile for no reason?"

"Teenage girls never smile for no reason. I think someone's in love."

When Mom says it all plainly like that, my heart speeds up as if she's just confessed my biggest, deepest secret. My love for Park isn't a secret and I'd never be ashamed of it, but this is my mother who's talking about it. Awkward.

What's even worse is the next few words out of my mouth. "I guess I'm just smiling because I realized he's the one."

"The one?" Mom says, placing a terrifying amount of meaning on that one individual word. "What makes you think Park is the one? You're only nineteen."

I shrug. "You knew Dad was the one when you were sixteen."

"No I didn't."

My mouth falls open and I stare at her waiting to see her laugh and tell me she's joking. When she doesn't, I say, "But you and Dad have been together since you were sixteen. At least that's the story I've been told my whole life..."

"We were, honey. We were high school sweethearts. But that doesn't mean I knew he was the one back then. I didn't know until I was much older."

"Well you stayed with him the whole time, so it's kind of the same thing."

Mom dries her hands on a dishtowel and pats my arm. "If Park is the real deal for you then I'm excited for you. But don't worry too much about putting labels on him. If it doesn't work out the way it did for your father and me, that doesn't mean anything. I want you to be happy."

"Thanks, Mom," I say. Now that a sufficient amount of awkward chit-chat has filled the room, I am dying for a subject change. "So when will dinner be ready?"

Chapter 8

I got the email two hours ago. I've been avoiding it like the bad omen that it probably is, wishing it would just disappear from my inbox and never resurface in my life.

With November here already, the air is colder, crisper and somehow more annoying than ever. Nothing in my closet looks good and I wonder how I got through last winter with such a pathetic wardrobe. Then it hits me. Park wasn't here last winter. I was able to go days without shaving my legs and I wore the same three sweatpants on rotation every day of the week. When I wasn't wearing my paint pants of course.

The paint pants are an old pair of yoga pants that I once got paint on while I was making a canvas. Now I wear them almost every time I paint, just in case I spill anything.

Last winter was easy when it came to finding clothes to wear. However, it was the hardest winter ever emotionally. I missed him like crazy. His racing schedule was hectic and I barely saw him for Christmas.

Now this year he's here for good, and all of the time. As much as I love seeing that boy every day, right now my closet is looking pretty dreary.

In an effort to prolong picking out something to wear, I grab my phone again and look at the stupid email. Midterm grades are in. I'm only taking two classes this semester, both because I suck, and because my parents had some massive house expenses to fix last summer and couldn't afford to pay for more classes. Not that I minded. I hate college.

I know I need to get it over with, rip off the proverbial bandage and see what kind of grades I'm making so I'll know if I need to drop a class. Or two. When I click the link and see my grades load, I'm not exactly sure how I feel.

I'm passing both classes, but barely. As I'm contemplating how pissed my parents would be if I dropped out of school forever, my phone gets a new email message. I have another sale on Etsy.

A familiar feeling falls over me as I read through the email, noticing that the buyer has purchased two canvasses. It's the same feeling, the same nagging idea that's been bothering me every single time I make a new sale. The idea that maybe I should just quit school, cut back my hours at C&C and focus on painting full time.

It's crazy, right? I can't possibly think this is a smart idea.

But it feels like a smart idea. My inspirational quote canvases have been selling almost as quickly as I can list them, and it's been steady since day one. This could be a thing. This could be my thing. I scroll back through my emails to the one that displays my class grades. Community college isn't all it's cracked up to be. Maybe some people do well in these stupid mandatory classes and then go on to be super successful business people who sit in a cubicle all day and stare at a computer and so business work.

That's never going to be me. I'll never survive a cubicle job. I need to be creative, to keep moving, keep dreaming, keep making beautiful things.

Scowling at the grades email, I swipe back to the new sale email. On the bottom of the invoice, the buyer has written me a message in the notes section.

I'm so excited to get these for my office wall! PS – do you do custom work? I'd love to have my company's slogan painted on a canvas. The girls in my office are going nuts for #BeccasInspirations!

I frown. Are people so obsessed with using hashtags that they now use them in random conversations? She does know this is an email and I can't actually click on it, right? My stomach fills up with butterflies as an insane idea comes to me. Maybe the hashtag symbol wasn't some kind of mistake. Maybe…

I find the Instagram app on my phone and open it, going straight to the search feature. I type in #BeccasInspirations and gasp. There are already forty-two images with that tag, all of them are of my artwork. One has a picture of a girl holding up her canvas and smiling. The caption reads: This quote motivates me so much! I LOVE IT #BeccasInspirations

Another user has posted a screenshot of a canvas on my Etsy page, saying they want to buy that canvas for their sister's wedding gift. I look at every single picture and read the comments, finding that all of them are positive and sweet. Not a single person has said anything like: These canvases are dumb and pointless. I hope the artist doesn't quit her day job. #BeccasInspirations

My cell phone screen gets blurry and I realize I'm shaking with the buildup of emotions inside of me right now. Not only are random strangers buying my art, they are talking about it on social media.

Maybe my dream isn't so stupid after all.

When Park calls me in the afternoon, he sounds exhausted. "Hey there, beautiful," he breathes into the phone as if he'd just finished a hundred yard dash.

"What's wrong?" I ask.

I hear the beeping sound of his truck's door being opened while the keys are in the ignition. "Just worn out," he says, pausing to take a drink. "Jace and I have been looking at some land and I just walked like a thousand miles through knee-high grass."

"Why are you looking at land? You just bought and house."

He hesitates for a moment and I can almost picture the face he makes as he contemplates telling me the truth or making up a lie. So I beat him to the punch. "Tell me the truth, boy."

He laughs. "Well...I was going to tell you about this in a more ... exciting ... atmosphere."

Okay, now I'm curious. "What does that mean?"

"Trust me, it's cool and you'll like it. But can it wait until dinner? Jace wants us to double date and tell our old ladies the good news at the same time."

"So Bayleigh and I are old ladies now, hmm?"

"Hey, those were Jace's words, not mine."

"Okay fine, I'll wait. So what else is up?"

"I don't know, you tell me. You sound like you have a secret yourself."

I bite my lip and clutch the phone tighter. He knows me so well. But I don't know why I'm so worried about telling him my idea—it's a good idea. I take a deep breath so that I can let it all out at once. "I'm selling a lot of artwork and I just found out that people are talking about me online and they like my work and I kind of hate college and I'm thinking I should just drop out and focus on my business."

"Wow. How did you say all of that in one breath?"

I sigh into the phone. "Seriously? Is that all you have to say?"

"No, Becca, I'm sorry. I was just playing around."

I hadn't even realized my heart was pounding until I take a deep breath and feel like I'm running a marathon. Even though this is my life, Park's thoughts on it really matter to me. Maybe I'm just delusional. I need some confirmation that this could be a good idea. "Well?" I ask impatiently.

"You really want my opinion?"

I nod and then realize he can't see me. "Yes, I do."

"I think you should do more than just paintings. You should take your most popular designs and sell digital prints, stickers, coffee mugs, stuff like that. Put your designs on T-shirts and handbags and stuff. The world likes your art and you could set all of that up online without having to paint more canvases."

"That sounds like…like you're encouraging me…"

"Of course I'm encouraging you. I'm very much a 'follow my heart' kind of person. If that's what you want to do, do it. I'll support you."

"You're the best," I say with a smile.

"Hey," he says suddenly.

"Yes?"

"I miss you."

"I miss you, babe."

"I mean I miss you, miss you." I can almost see his eyebrows wiggling in that suggestive way that makes my stomach flutter.

"Maybe we can remedy that," I whisper into the phone, hoping that I sound at least a little bit sexy.

"I hope so."

Chapter 9

The remedy comes quickly. Ollie calls me just a few minutes after I get off the phone with Park and tells me that C&C BMX Park will be closed down tonight, courtesy of a transformer outage that left the facility without power. The power company will have it up and running by tomorrow morning, but for now, I'm free.

It's only four p.m. when I get the good news, and I decide to surprise Park with my company. He had said he was planning on cooking a frozen pizza for dinner, so I know he'll be home. Nervous is about the most underrated word in the world to describe how I feel as I shower and get ready to drive over to his house. I use the fancy conditioner so my hair will look great, and I shave my legs…twice. I want tonight to be perfect because you never know if it'll be the night.

I'm so excited and anxious to see him that I don't bother going through every outfit in my closet to deliberate on them—I just grab something quickly. Luckily, that something I chose was a form-fitting pair of ripped up jeans and a black tank top with rhinestone decorations along the neckline. If the cleavage on this shirt happens to make my boobs look awesome well…that's just a random coincidence.

Knowing that boy can eat an entire frozen pizza by himself, I stop at the grocery store and grab another pizza, a dozen brownies from the bakery and a two liter of Coke. The whole time I'm shopping and driving to his place, Park is texting me silly things about how much he misses me and how he can't wait to see me. Even with those texts as confirmation, I'm still freaking out when I arrive at his house.

His truck is the only vehicle in the driveway and that makes me oddly relieved. It would have been awkward to stumble upon a party I wasn't invited to.

Then, of course, of course—as soon as I'm feeling good about surprising Park with dinner and brownies, he doesn't answer the door. I knock again, feeling increasingly stupid as I hold a bag of food and stand on his front porch. When he doesn't answer, I take out my phone and shoot him a text.

Me: So...what are you doing?

Less than a minute later, he replies.

Park: Playing Xbox. How's work?

I smile. I know how that boy plays Xbox—loud as hell and taking up all of his attention. He's probably in his bedroom upstairs and can't even hear me knocking on the door. Because he's unknowingly scared the crap out of me, I decide to play a little game with him too.

Me: I have a problem...

Park: What? Are you okay?

Me: No...

My phone rings. Leave it to Park to insist on having important conversations on the phone. I answer and try not to laugh. "Hello?"

"Babe, are you okay? What happened?"

"Calm down, it's nothing big," I say with a smile. "I just have this little problem."

"And what is that?"

"My boyfriend won't answer the door."

All I can hear are shuffling sounds and then the heavy footfalls of Park running down the wooden staircase. The front door clicks and then swings wide open. Park takes one look at me, my bag of food, and the lopsided grin on my face. Then he swoops me into his arms.

My bag drops to the floor just inside of the living room. I squeal. He buries his lips into the crook of my neck and kisses me repeatedly, making me laugh uncontrollably. Then he pulls away and kisses me on the lips, right where I need him to kiss.

"I missed you," he whispers, cupping my face in his hands. Before I can tell him that I missed him too, he crushes his lips over mine and slides his hands down my body, gripping me around the waist. I grab his shoulders, digging my fingers into him as he pulls me closer to him.

When I come up for air, he pulls me up, up, up, until I'm eye level with him and my feet are hanging in the air. I wrap them around his waist and he slides his hands into my back pockets, holding me firmly against his chest. My toes tingle and my heart races and forehead presses against his. "I missed you too," I whisper.

"The more time I spend with you the more I know I can't live without you."

I smile, too love-drunk to bother saying anything. Instead of talking, I just grip his shoulders and lean into him, soaking up every second of this moment. My eyes close and he moves, carrying me with him. When I feel a step, I lift up and open my eyes. "Where are we go—Park!" I wriggle but he holds me tighter. "Oh my God, you can't walk up stairs with me."

He smirks. "Why not?"

"I'm too heavy!" It would be entirely too embarrassing if my weight made us both tumble down the stairs.

Park makes this arrogant snort as we round the corner of the staircase halfway up to the second floor. "You are nowhere near being too heavy, miss."

When we get to his bedroom, he lowers me onto the bed. Only he doesn't have a real bed yet, so it's an air mattress. At least he's had time to put a new set of sheets on top of it. I'm pretty sure my heart is pounding so hard that it's nearing the point of exploding, but I take a deep breath and run my fingers through Park's hair as he hovers over me.

Moments like this are so powerful, so full of love and bliss and an insane amount of adrenaline. We make out, lips crashing together, tongues grazing, bodies pressed together. I don't even realize when my hands have slid so far up Park's shirt that he leans back and pulls it off his head, tossing it to the floor.

Slowly, he lowers back down, bracing himself above me with his hands on the bed on either side of my head. This position makes his biceps look freaking huge and his chest — well his chest is always perfect. I can't help myself when my fingers trail over his abs, up to his chest and then back down again.

"I love you," I say.

"Are you talking to me or my abs?" he asks.

I roll my eyes. "Both."

"I'm cool with that." He kisses me again, and my hands find their way around his waist and up his back. Every movement that brings him closer to me, makes me the warmth in my stomach turn to fire.

Park leans on one hand and slides the other one up my shirt, slowly, purposely. I get chills at the touch of his warm hand over my skin. He rests his thumb and index finger just under my bra, and then he makes eye contact with me and rubs his thumb over my breast. I squirm in the best way possible and pull him closer to me, digging my hips upward into his.

"Mmm," Park groans. I bite my lip and pull him down to me, kissing him harder than before. The next thing I know, my shirt is gingerly pulled over my head and tossed on top of the other shirt on the floor.

Exposed, I feel a wave of nervous excitement and then immediately blush when Park doesn't hide the fact that he's checking out my body. Even though I still have a bra on, I can't help but squirm. He holds me in place and leans down, kissing the top of my breast and then moving to the other one, trailing soft kisses over my skin. He leans back, sitting on his heels as he straddles me. He dips his thumbs into the waistband of my jeans and slides them across my hips. The sensation makes me gasp as a rolling tingle of pleasure settles in my stomach. Then, instead of going lower, his hands—his warm amazing hands—slide up my stomach and cup my breasts. He squeezes them and kisses my cleavage, grinding his hips into mine.

"Oh my god," I moan, throwing my head back and grinding back into him.

"Do you…" Park says, his voice raspy between his ragged breathing. "Do you want to…?"

"What?" I ask a second before the answer comes tumbling down on me like a pile of bricks. He's talking about sex. My throat dries up and the uncomfortable panic I feel must show in my face because Park climbs off of me and rolls over on the air mattress.

"It's okay, baby." He brushes a hand through my hair. "We don't have to."

"I want to, I just…" I swallow and try to think of the right words. I mean, does he even have protection? Should I bring some next time? Isn't it supposed to hurt? Ugh. I can't say any of that out loud.

Park places a kiss on my forehead. "We can take our time. There's no rush."

"Thanks," I manage to say even though my throat has totally dried up and my heart is no longer beating. Embarrassment fills every inch of my body. "I'm sorry, I—"

Park shakes his head. "No. No sorry, no regret. It's just sex, babe. We'll do it when you're ready."

I sigh and look away, unable to say anything because I'm so freaking embarrassed. Maybe I should just be single for the rest of my life so I'll never have to feel this way again. I bet he's never been denied before—not with other girls. California girls. Girls who aren't me.

Chapter 10

Work is swamped with BMX kids the next day. I don't know if it's because we were closed yesterday, but today we have at least twice as many riders as normal. It's also getting colder outside, now that it's November so people are probably finding indoor activities to do instead of face the cold. Whatever the case, I can't even take a coffee break until noon. And at noon, I no longer want coffee. I want lunch.

"Olllllie," I whine, slumping across the front counter as if I'm in the middle of acting out an elaborate death scene. "I'm hungryyyy."

"So go to lunch!" he says, appearing from his office which is off to the side of the front desk. "You've been busy all morning, you could use a break."

I stand up and frown. "Yeah, but look around. It's way too busy to leave. I can't leave you here all by yourself."

"Sure you can. I'll survive."

I sigh, glance at the coffee maker in his office and then back out at the massive BMX park behind me. Maybe I could just power up on caffeine and skip lunch, or take a late lunch if it ever does slow down. Or... "Hey, let's just order pizza and have them deliver it."

Ollie glances over at me, taking his eyes off of the spreadsheet on his computer for the first time all morning. "Now that's a good idea."

"Sweet," I say, feeling as if I've solved some epic world problem. "I'll order pizza."

I spin around from Ollie's office to the front desk, where I grab the business phone before I look up at the customer that just walked in.

"No need to order pizza," the customer says. Wait. That's not a customer.

I drop the phone and scurry around the front counter, where Park awaits, bags of takeout food in his hands. "Babe!" I squeal, throwing my arms around him. He can't hug me back because his hands are full, but he leans his head on mine in what can be considered an armless hug. "Why are you here? I thought you were busy today?"

After I had gone home last night, Park and I stayed up on the phone for another hour and he had explained that although he had exciting news to tell me about what he and Jace had been up to lately, he couldn't share it with me until after today. Today was a big deal and he said he'd probably be busy until late in the afternoon. The curiosity has been killing me, but after your boyfriend quits his professional career, moves across the country and buys a house, pretty much nothing else he does can be considered surprising.

Park sets the bags on the counter and leans over it to wave at Ollie from the opening of his office door. "Ol, I brought Chinese food."

My boss lets out a whoop because we all know he loves Chinese food. Park gives me a look of enthusiasm, and although he's not actually bouncing on his heels like a child on Christmas morning, the look in his eyes says he's just as excited.

"What is it?" I ask, peering up at him suspiciously. "You're here when you're supposed to be busy, and you're smiling like you have…" I take a guess, "Good news?"

He nods, biting his lower lip. "Very good news."

I lift an eyebrow. "How good?"

"Well, let's just say it makes up for quitting my job."

Park joins me behind the front counter and we dig into our food. Luckily, it's finally getting slow at work so I don't have to do that weird shuffle of pretending I'm not eating when customers come inside. I open a container of eggrolls. "Okay, now that my stomach is no longer trying to eat itself, tell me about this good news."

Park smiles and stares at me for a weirdly long time. "I think it's good news. I hope you do, too."

"Okay, now I'm scared."

"Don't be scared. It's just a lot. Jace and I are taking on a lot of stuff here and I want you to be cool with it because I want us to be cool."

"We are cool," I say. "As a cucumber."

"Oh my God, you're a dork."

I point my half-eaten eggroll at him. "Tell me the news!"

He takes a deep breath and stands a little straighter. "Well...since Jace got kicked out of professional racing, he's been working at Mixon Motocross Park giving lessons to other riders."

"I know this, but what does it have to do with you?" I ask, a bit impatiently.

"And now that I've quit, I've been thinking that teaching young riders all of my amazing knowledge would be a fun thing."

"Have you actually worked with kids?" I interject, tossing a look over my shoulder to indicate the kids on BMX bikes behind us. "Kids kind of suck."

He shakes his head. "Not motocross kids. Anyhow, Mixon is a little too small for Jace to keep doing this as a full time job, and they're a racing track first of all so a lot of times the races are getting in his way of taking on new clients. And I need a job, so Jace and I have been collaborating on buying some land down here and opening a facility that's just dedicated to training people in motocross. No races to get in the way."

"Like a training camp?" I ask.

He nods. "We were thinking of having actual camps, too. Like in the summer, we could do a week-long camp where kids come to ride every day and practice their skills. We can teach hole shots, jumps, tricks, cornering—all kinds of stuff. It'll keep me in the sport of motocross but I won't have to travel anymore and I can stay here with you. Make a life with you."

The last part he said sends chills down my spine. "I think this is a really great idea," I say, temporarily ignoring that last thing he had said. Making a life with me implies too much, is too emotional, too important. But the job thing? That's a good idea. "It'll be really good for Jace, too since he has a family now. What does Mr. Fisher think about this?"

Mr. Fisher is the owner of Mixon Motocross Park and Jace's boss. He's been supportive of Jace so far in his career transition and I'm pretty sure it was his idea to hire Jace as a trainer at the track. Park smiles. "Mr. Fisher is totally on board. He wants to be an investor."

"An investor? Wow. That's fancy business talk," I say, poking my boyfriend in the ribs. He grabs my hand and kisses it quickly before letting it go. "I know. It's a big deal. That's what Jace and I have been doing lately, getting all the business stuff in order. We've been looking at land and we found a great place that's between Lawson and Mixon. It's about sixteen acres and it has a pond in one corner of the land which would be great for watering the track."

"Wow," I say. "So...that's where you went this morning?"

He nods. "We made an offer on the land. And they accepted our offer immediately."

My eyes go wide. "Seriously? You just bought sixteen acres of land?"

"With Jace. We're both half-owners. Mr. Fisher is lending us his equipment to rip up the land and build a few tracks and jumps for it. After a while, we're hoping to earn enough money to buy our own tractors and stuff."

"Park, this is a big deal," I say, but it's more of a thought to myself. Lately I've been thinking of expanding my art and trying to create a business for myself with it. Now Park is taking that leap himself, making a business out of something he loves. "It might be crazy, but I think it could work."

"I think so, too." Park stabs his fork into his rice and then takes both of my hands in his. "It's risky and it'll be a lot of hard work, but Jace and I have made names for ourselves in the motocross world. People know who we are and they know we're skilled. I've already talked to dozens of amateur racers and their parents and these people are willing to pay to have professional racers teach their kids. But I need your support, babe."

"Of course you have my support," I say, lifting up on my toes and kissing him.

From the side office, I hear Ollie yell, "Gross!" but I know he's just messing with us. I look back at him and stick out my tongue.

As soon as my work shift is over, I check my emails and find that I've sold six paintings in the last hour alone. I don't even have to do the math to know that my piddly part-time hourly wages at C&C don't even come close to what I'm earning with my paintings. If I were to quit my job and focus solely on my art, then I'd earn more than my paychecks are now.

Hell, I'm already earning more than my paychecks are now. I drive home and think about all of the things Park told me earlier today. He and his best friend are taking a leap, starting a company, and changing their destinies. They want something and they're going for it.

I'm battling my own career ideas, too. I hate college, I love my art. The choice should be simple. But I feel overwhelmingly guilty when I think about quitting college. Mom and dad would probably be pissed. Actually, scratch the probably. They would be totally pissed.

At a red light, I lean my head against the headrest in my car and stare at the roof. Why is being an adult so freaking hard? Why can't I just throw caution to the wind and follow my dreams like Park and Jace are doing?

I've legally been an adult for two years now. But I don't feel like one. I mean, I still live with my parents and I'm still a virgin. It seems like everything in life is going on, growing up and taking control of life while I'm just sitting here idly wishing I could do things but not actually doing any of them.

By the time I get home, I don't feel any more empowered about my future.

In fact, I feel smaller than ever.

Chapter 11

I've just done something really stupid.

Last night, after wallowing in my own insecurities, I had stayed up until two in the morning making art. I painted every single canvas I had left, all fourteen of them. I spent an extra hour going through my quotes notebook and searching the internet for more inspiring things to paint on future canvasses. In my sleep-deprived state, and probably slightly high from all the paint fumes, I had made a decision. I was going to quit college.

Mom was awake in the living room, binge-watching a show on Netflix that she'd recently become so obsessed with that she often stayed up late into the night watching more episodes. Armed with confidence and paint fumes, I had marched into the living room, looked her straight in the eyes and said, "Mom, I'm quitting college."

She snorted and looked back at her television. "Get to sleep, Becca. You've lost your mind."

I was so tired, I did what she said without complaint.

Now, it's ten in the morning on a Wednesday. I shuffle down the hallway and into the kitchen to make myself a bowl of cereal. I'm off work and school today since I only have classes on Tuesdays and Thursdays. It's a perfect day for lounging around and doing nothing.

Mom sits at the kitchen island eating some yogurt and reading the newspaper. "Good morning," she says with a yawn.

"Hey." It would be easy to continue on with my day acting as if everything is fine and pretending that last night didn't happen. But that's what the old Becca would do. I wasn't out of my mind last night. I've never been more sure of something in my whole life.

If Jace and Park can quit their careers and start a business, then I can find it in me to quit college, which currently isn't doing anything for my future and start up a business that is already earning good money. If I fail, then I fail. I can always go back to college. But I really want to try this out now, while Becca's Inspirations are selling like crazy.

"Mom, can we talk?"

My mother's eyes bulge as she sips her coffee quickly and then sets the coffee cup down with a clink. "Of course," she says. I can see it now: her head is filling with all the horrors of what I could possibly say next. Mom, I'm pregnant. Mom, I'm in big trouble with the mafia. Mom, I totally crashed your car into a retirement home and killed a dozen nice old ladies.

I smile to ease her fears a bit. "Remember last night?" She nods. "Um, I wasn't joking about it. I really want to quit college. At least for a little bit."

She takes another sip of coffee. "Why is that?"

Suddenly the well-rehearsed speech I had formed in my mind while making my cereal is gone. Totally erased from my memory by the power of Mom's piercing stare. "Well...I'm not doing so well in my classes," I begin.

Mom shrugs. "You get the same degree with C's as you do with A's. As long as you're passing, who cares?

"That's just it, Mom. I'm going for a general studies associate's degree. You can't exactly get a job with that, and right now I'm not doing great in my classes and I kind of hate it. I think I can have a better career with my art."

"I'm listening." Those are the words Mom says to me, but the look on her face indicates the exact opposite.

"I'm making money with my art."

"Honey, artists never make money. That's exactly where the term 'starving artist' comes from."

I take out my phone and open up my Etsy store to the page with how much money I've made this month. "I made almost two thousand dollars last month and I'm already at fifteen hundred now. The month is only half over so I might end up with three thousand dollars."

"Wow. That's impressive, honey." She scrolls through the website on my phone. "You should charge more than thirty five dollars though."

"That's what Park thinks too. I'll consider it." Hopefully by agreeing with her, she'll see things my way. After a few minutes of me nervously watching her look through my Etsy account, she slides the phone back to me. "Don't you think it's a good idea?" I ask.

"No."

"But, Mom—I'm making a lot of money. If I quit college I can work harder on my art and sell even more. Park thinks I should expand into prints on coffee mugs and stuff."

"I absolutely agree that you should expand your business, but honey you take two classes just two days a week. Work on your art during the other five days."

I stir my spoon around in my cereal which is now so soggy I don't want to eat it. "But Mom, I hate college."

"I don't care, Becca. Your father and I are paying for you to get an education and that's what you're going to do. Stop sighing like that."

I close my eyes and bite my tongue. The last thing I need to do is get into an argument with my mom, but I was really hoping she'd be more open to the idea. "You know this is my dream, right?" I say, in one last desperate bid to win her over to my way of thinking. "Isn't that the whole point of life? Following your dreams. Finding what makes you happy and doing it? I've found that, Mom. It's my art. I don't need a college degree to create something that people want to buy."

"Even so, you'll need a business degree to run your own business. You'll need education on taxes and bookkeeping. All of that is something you learn in college, not by following your gut."

"What if I just take a year off?" I ask. She gets up and pours herself another cup of coffee and I expand on my idea. "Just one year away from college so I can focus on my art and if it takes off like I want it to, then I'll go back to college. And if it doesn't, and these last two months were just a fluke, then I'll know and at least I would have tried. Then I'll go back to college. See? It works out both ways."

It's a lie. It's a total lie and I hope Mom doesn't see it that way. The truth is, if I succeed with my art, I'll be able to hire someone to do my bookkeeping and my taxes. If I end up making a living with my art, then I will do what's best for me when it's time for it. But Mom doesn't need to know all of that. She just needs to agree to let me drop out.

"Honey, I appreciate your effort here, but you're not quitting college. As long as you live under my roof, you will attend Lawson Community College."

Since Park is meeting with Jace all day to work on their new business, I rode with him to Mixon to hang out with Bayleigh. The boys are in the living room with paperwork and calculators and we're in Bayleigh's room, playing with Jett.

Bayleigh's eyes light up when I recount the talk with my mom from this morning. "Looks like we know what that means," she says, punching my arm playfully.

"It means I'm freaking screwed," I mutter.

"No..." She draws out the word so long that I look up at her and lift an eyebrow.

"Uh, yes?" I say. "She's not going to let me quit college."

"She said not while you're under her roof."

"Trust me, I heard that part loud and clear. But even if I make three thousand dollars a month, there's no guarantee I'll make that every month plus I have to pay taxes on it and there's no way I could afford my own apartment and all the bills that come with it." I sigh and rest my head in my hands. Even Jett's adorable baby smile doesn't cheer me up right now. "I'll be living with my parents for a while. That means I'm stuck in college."

"Okay first of all, you're lucky because I want to go to college and I can't until Jett is older, and secondly, you're totally missing the point, Becca." She points toward her bedroom door, signaling to where the boys are in the living room. "You don't have to pay your own apartment bills. You just have to share them with someone."

"You mean Park?" I ask. The very idea of living with Park makes me lightheaded. "I don't know about that."

"Don't tell me you guys haven't talked about you moving in yet? I mean, hello! He just bought a house! A man doesn't need that big freaking house all to himself."

"We've danced around the subject, but we haven't actually talked about it."

She leans into me with her shoulder. "Whyyyy not? Come on, Becca! Dooooo it."

I laugh. "It's not like I can just pack up my stuff and move in with him. He has to ask me and all of that."

She rolls her eyes. "Uh, yeah you can. Here I'll help you pack." She pretends to stand up. "Let's go get your stuff and move you in today."

"It's not like that. I kind of need the guy's permission first. Preferably, I'd like it if he asks me to move in. I don't want to be the kind of girl that begs to live with him."

"I get what you're saying and all of that, but you're not that kind of girl. Park is crazy about you and I know he'd be psyched if you moved in with him."

Before I speak, I make sure to lower my voice just in case anyone happens to be walking by the door. "It's easy for you to say that because you have this perfect fairytale romance thing going on. I can't ask him to let me move in. He has to ask me on his own."

"He'll ask."

"I hope so." I smile and think about the guy who has captured my heart and is currently hanging out on the other side of Bayleigh's apartment. There's no doubt in my mind that he's the guy I want with me for the rest of my life.

Chapter 12

My dad has Thanksgiving off work for the first time in forever, so my parents go all out to celebrate the holiday. Instead of buying a pre-cooked turkey from the market like usual, Mom actually cooks one herself, making the stuffing from scratch and everything. I participate in the same way I do every year, by making the pies. One pumpkin, one apple and one chocolate. I don't have a favorite—they are all equally delicious.

This is my second Thanksgiving as a couple with Park, but it's the first one we've been able to spend together. Mom invited him over for dinner but Dad said he should come over early to watch football. My parents both really like Park, but that doesn't stop my anxiety levels from going through the roof the moment he arrives.

I rush to the front door the second the doorbell rings. I've seen my boyfriend a million times but on this occasion, it feels like a first date all over again. My fingers fumble with opening the door, and when I do, I'm greeted first by a bouquet of flowers.

"Happy Thanksgiving, love." Park leans in for a quick kiss on my cheek and I take the flowers he gives me.

"Thanksgiving isn't a flower-giving occasion, you know," I tease him as I let him into the foyer and close the door behind us.

"When you're dating a cop's daughter, every occasion is a flower-giving occasion."

He takes off his suede jacket, revealing a black long-sleeved button up shirt that fits him as if it was tailored to his muscles. Instantly, I feel underdressed in my teal knee-length dress with a shimmery overlay of lace.

"Park is here!" I call out to my parents as we walk into the kitchen. Dad yells for Park to join him in the living room and Mom showers him with offers of food and drink. Okay, so maybe this day won't be as awkward as I had imagined.

During dinner, Park acts like a total gentleman. It's almost as if he's an entirely different person from the laid back guy I know. He's proper and polite and eats with a fork and a knife. I'm weirdly proud of him, of the guy I've brought home to meet my parents and how well put together he is.

I kind of want to shout, "See, Mom and Dad? Park quit his job and started a business and you love him! Why can't you let me do the same thing?" But I don't. I'm smarter than that.

Dad asks about Park's house and how the renovations are going. They talk about flooring and air conditioning and Dad offers to help him with repairs. Everything is going really well, better than I could have expected. And after dinner, everyone, including my mom who is perpetually on a diet, likes all three of my pies. It turns out that eating a slice of each on one plate is the actual definition of heaven.

"So, Park," Dad says, throwing an arm around his shoulder as he walks us to the front door. Mom and Dad have agreed to let me out of family Thanksgiving early to go see a movie with Park. "In the last few months, you've moved away from your home down and came all the way here to Texas. That's a big life change."

"Yes, sir it was." Park doesn't skip a beat. "It was the right move for my career."

"Uh, huh," Dad says. "And did Becca have maybe a small part in your decision?"

Park doesn't hide the emotion in his eyes when he replies. "Yes, sir. She certainly had a lot to do with it."

Chapter 13

While the rest of the nation crams into super long lines at four in the morning on the Friday after Thanksgiving, Bayleigh and I have a better idea. We do our Christmas shopping on December first. It's after the stupid Black Friday rush of idiocy, at least that's what Bayleigh calls it, and it's before the stores get insanely packed with Christmas shoppers.

December first is the perfect date for holiday shopping.

Now, if only I knew what to get Park.

Last year had been easy. Park's favorite band, Zombie Radio, had a gig in Houston and I'd managed to score backstage meet and green passes along with front row seats. It had taken two weeks of listening to the radio and calling in thirty million times, but my dedication had paid off. It was a free present, but Park said it was the best one he'd ever gotten.

Trying to find a way to top that gift this year will be next to impossible.

"Why don't you just give him the gift of sex?" Bayleigh suggests. "You can't beat that."

"Oh my God, shut up," I say, rolling my eyes as I find a great parking spot just outside of the mall. My shopping list today includes about a million toys for Jett, and collector's addition box set of the Blood Crave series by Christina

Channelle for Mom. She's obsessed with young adult books and that's her favorite author, so she should love it.

Dad's gift will be a new wallet for his police badge since the one he has now is all worn out and looks like it's survived through about twenty apocalypses. For Bayleigh, I'm getting her a gift card to Victoria's Secret (which is what we get each other every year) and as many bottles of nail polish as I can fit into one shopping bag at Sephora.

I'm not exactly sure what I'll get Ollie, but I know it'll be in the form of some kind of t-shirt at his favorite surf shop in the mall. I have everyone figured out and accounted for; everyone except for the most important guy in my life right now.

I sigh as we walk inside the mall. Bayleigh has been talking this entire time but I haven't even heard a word she's said, thanks to being caught up in my own world of obsessing over Park. I smile and nod at her and she keeps talking, totally unaware of how much of a bad friend I am. Good. She doesn't need to know that I'm so pathetic I can't even put Park out of my mind for five minutes.

After a few hours of shopping, my best friend and I have a dozen bags between the two of us, and we're all shopped out. Everyone on my list is accounted for except for Park, and it's been a pretty good day despite that.

Since I'm driving, I take Bayleigh over to her mom's house so we can pick up Jett and I can't help myself—I give him one of the toys I had picked out for him at the surf shop. It's a stuffed shark and he loves it. It's official. I am the coolest godmother around.

When I get home later, I drop off all of my presents and hide them in the back of my closet. Three of my paintings sold while we were at the mall, so I find the right canvases and pack them up with a shipping label to drop off at the post office before heading to Park's house.

This is the first Christmas of my life where I'm not worried about needing money to buy gifts. And now, that I have literally hundreds of dollars that I could use on a gift for Park, I can't think of a single thing to get him.

When I get there, I let myself in because the front door is wide open. "Park?" I call out from the foyer.

"Be there in a second," he calls out from somewhere upstairs. I walk toward the staircase and get there right when Park comes barreling down them, covered in sweat and wearing a smile the size of Texas. "Hey there," he says.

I go to rush into his arms, but immediately stop when my hands get soaked against his back. "Ugh," I say, stepping back.

Park laughs. "Sorry, I was working on the house."

"Well hurry and shower because I need some massive cuddle time."

His eyebrows draw together. "Is everything okay?"

I nod. "I am stressed out about something but it's not a big deal."

"What is it?"

I push him gently with my hands. "Shower first. Talk later."

Hours later, we're cuddled on the couch and I've just poured my heart out to him. "Seriously? Christmas presents?" he says, gently stroking my hair with his fingers. "You seemed really upset earlier and it was just because you don't know what to get me?" He shakes his head and laughs as if that's the silliest reason to be upset.

Okay, so, maybe I didn't tell him everything.

"Yeah," I say. "My present last year was so great and this year I can't think of anything to get you. You're a guy who doesn't really want many things."

He squeezes me closer and grabs the remote to turn down the volume. "You're all I need."

"You can't say that. I want to get you something. But there's no way I can top last year's present."

"Every year doesn't have to top the year before it, babe. If you really want to blow me away this Christmas…" He places a finger to his lips as if he's concentrating and he looks around the living room. "I need dishes, a welcome mat for the front door, some more towels...basically anything for this house and I'd be psyched."

"So maybe I'll just get you a nice toaster and call it a day," I say with a laugh.

"I like toast. That would work."

I roll my eyes. "I have to give you something good." Then, because I'm a little insane with anxiety over the sex topic, and because I'd like to judge his reaction, I muster up some boldness and say, "Maybe I'll cover myself with whipped cream and give you myself as a present."

"Mmmm," he says, tucking his lips in the space between my head and shoulder. "That would be the present of the century."

"Would that count as a present?" I ask lightly, as if it's a joke. It is so not a joke.

"It'd be the best present ever."

All the blood in my entire body rushes to my cheeks as I say, "I'll see what I can do."

Chapter 14

The smell of Mom's delicious lasagna makes my mouth water as I put the finishing touches on my family's presents. Mom always makes a lasagna for Christmas Eve dinner. The tradition in our family is as old as I am. Dad always works Christmas day for the double overtime pay and we celebrate on Christmas Eve.

As a kid it was awesome because I got all my presents from Mom and Dad a day early and then I woke up to even more presents from Santa Claus. Now the magic of Santa is gone, but I find more joy in seeing my parents open their gifts now that I'm old enough to afford some.

This year I went a little overboard with the gift buying, but I couldn't help myself since I have so much money at the moment. My paintings have been selling like crazy, probably thanks to the Christmas rush, and I have over six thousand dollars in my account. Mom almost lost her mind when I said I'd like to start paying for my cell phone and car insurance bill. It just doesn't feel right letting my parents pay for stuff when I'm almost twenty years old and can actually afford it myself.

I cap the pen I had used to write "from Santa" and "from Aunt Becca" on the gift tags for Jett's presents. Then I adorn the boxes of colorfully wrapped presents with sparkly bows.

Now I can smell the garlic bread from the kitchen, so I know dinner is almost ready. I grab Mom and Dad's presents, which ended up being six gifts for each of them, and rush them out to put under the tree, leaving behind Jett and Bayleigh's gifts, and of course, Park's.

I went a little overboard for Park, too. I got him the toaster, some silverware, a blender for those shakes he likes but never makes because he doesn't have a blender, a motocross themed shower curtain and bathmat, and some curtains for his bedroom because the moonlight is crazy bright from where the gigantic windows that face his bed.

And then, well, I accidently bought him more gifts. Flannel pajama pants, some button up shirts for meeting with future clients, the season DVDs of his favorite show, and a framed picture of the two of us, my favorite picture we've ever taken. We were at the beach with Jace and Bayleigh, it was cold outside so we were just walking along the sand. I was wearing a tan scarf I had just finished knitting and was very proud of it. Park wore a grey and white striped shirt that I picked out for him at a surf shop near the beach. He had to change clothes because a gust of wind had knocked me into him earlier, spilling half of my ice cream all over his other shirt.

It was the first time I had completely embarrassed myself in front of a guy and that guy had made me feel like it wasn't a big deal. He had ripped off his ice cream-soaked shirt and held my hand all the way to the nearest store to buy a new one. I still get chills when I picture how good his bare chest looked, lightly dotted with goosebumps because it was so cold outside. I had wanted to run my hand over his chest so bad, but didn't because we were in public and we hadn't been dating that long.

The picture was taken by Bayleigh after Park had a new shirt and I had jumped on his back, just playing around. I barely had time to register Bayleigh's words when she held up her phone and yelled, "Smile!"

Maybe it was the memories that day held, or maybe it was the way Park was looking up at me, smiling like he didn't have a care in the world. Whatever the case, it was my favorite picture of us, and I decided to make him a copy to keep in his new office.

The excess of gifts for Park wasn't because I suddenly have money this year. It was my way of making up for feeling so inadequate with the gift I really wanted to give him.

Myself.

After dinner and presents, my parents swear they don't mind if I go to Park's for a while, so I slip out of the house feeling only a little bit guilty about abandoning them on Christmas

Eve. I think the weirdest thing about leaving on Christmas Eve is the fact that they don't really seem to care at all. I'm no longer a child and although I'm very happy about that, it's also a little weird.

Park's presents hang out in the back seat of my car on the short drive to his new house. My whole car smells like the body wash I used profusely in my shower before I left the house tonight. My hair is also freshly washed and dried, my nails painted, my legs shaved. I need this night to be amazing and I'm not about to let some leg stubble ruin it.

My crazy hot boyfriend is sitting on the porch when I pull into the driveway. He sips from a mug of what is probably hot chocolate and gives me a little wave when I step out of the car.

"Do you have some of that for me?" I ask as I open the door to my backseat. "It's freezing out here."

"Of course I do. What are you doing?" he asks as he gets up and walks off the porch.

"Getting your presents," I call out from the backseat of my car. I try to fit them all in my hands at once, but that's so not happening.

Just as a couple of the gifts tumble out of my grasp, Park jumps to my rescue and catches them. "Oh my God, babe. You didn't have to get so many."

I roll my eyes. "How many did you get me?"

Guilt moves up his face until he bursts into a smile. "A lot."

Chapter 15

"Why won't you open them yet?" I whine, jutting out my bottom lip as we stare at the pile of presents I've dropped under his tiny Christmas tree. It's a fake tree, only about two feet tall and we found it in the attic of the house when he was moving it. So far we've decorated it with the antique ornaments that were also found in the attic and a strand of blue LED lights we got at the store.

"Because I want you to see your present first."

I put my hands on my hips. "Is it invisible?" I ask, because there's nothing under his tree except what I just put there.

Park's subtle smile widens. "Your present is definitely visible. It's just not right here."

"So…where is it?" I ask, walking toward him.

"Cold!" he says, and steps backward. I stop and turn to the right. "A little warmer," he says. I follow his cold and warm clues until I'm right in front of the staircase. "You're getting super super hot," he says. I take a few steps up the stairs. "Scalding."

I turn toward the second floor and he shakes his head. "Cold, again Sosa."

I can't believe it took me this long to figure it out, but I finally get it. I back up from the second floor landing and give him a coy smile. I point toward the ceiling. "Is it up here?" I ask.

Park bites his lip and nods. He's standing two steps below me on the stairs so I'm as tall as he is now. I lean forward and place a kiss on his cheek. "Is it in the room you've been keeping from me?" I whisper. He nods again.

I let out a little squeal and rush up the rest of the stairs to the room at the very top of the house. My hand touches the doorknob on the very door to the room I haven't been allowed to see yet. With great satisfaction, I twist and let it open.

My jaw drops. Not because the room is much bigger than I had pictured, with a bay window that stretches from one end to the other, but because of what's inside the room. Park had said it'd make a good paint studio. But now he's transformed it.

I step into the room feeling as if I'm in a dream, floating around instead of walking. The bay window has been refinished with a long bench pillow to sit on, and several new throw pillows in purple and teal and pink. I can't even fathom the idea of Park going to a store and picking these out, but he's done an amazing job. The window itself is adorned with a strand of little clear lights that give the room a charming glow. The hardwood flooring has a fluffy purple rug in the center of the room. One of my paintings, a canvas that simply says follow your dreams is hung on the wall.

But that's not even the best part.

In the middle of the room, facing the window, is an easel with a blank canvas already set up on the stand. A big red bow sits on the corner of the canvas and a table with fresh new paintbrushes, tons of paints in every color, and a collection of mixed media supplies rest in a neat line against the wall.

Park has taken little bits of the things I love, every aspect of what makes me happy, and turned it into a glorious paint studio just for me.

I don't even realize tears are in my eyes until I blink and they roll down my cheeks. I turn around and find Park standing in the doorway, a look of anxious anticipation on his face. "What do you think?" he says, gesturing to the room.

I crush into him, throwing my arms around his shoulders. He catches me, hoisting me up until I'm eye level with him and he's holding me in the air. I kiss him hard. "It's the best present ever," I say, burying my head into his shoulder. "My presents for you suck now."

"No they don't," he says, squeezing me to him, his calloused hands pressing into my back. "It's not a competition, anyhow."

I shake my head and wipe away the tears. "Hey...Park?"

"Mmm?" he says into my collarbone as his lips gently kiss me.

"Take me to your room." My request is a whisper, but he hears me and does exactly as he's told.

Chapter 16

I wrap my legs around my boyfriend's waist and cling to his neck as he descends the stairs much too quickly, in my opinion. I let out a frightened squeal as we round the corner banister to the second floor. "I got you," he says, sounding way too amused with himself. He may be strong enough to carry me, but one misstep could send us tumbling down two flights of stairs.

But he makes it to his bedroom door as promised, and shifts his hands to where one is wrapped around me and the other opens his bedroom door. He closes it behind us and although we're the only two people in the house, it feels much safer within the privacy of his bedroom.

Just like in the movie make out scenes, Park walks me to his bed and lowers me onto it. He doesn't even stumble. There's something so sexy about a man who can carry me around and set me on the bed without so much as gasping for breath.

"Come here," I whisper, and Park climbs onto the bed, on top of me, with his arms on either side of my head. I slip my hands under his shirt, planning on doing some kind of sexy slow motion movement to take it off, but the moment my fingers touch his warm muscular stomach, I can't help myself. I grab his shirt and pull it over his head and he helps me take his arms out.

Without waiting for him to make a move, I lift my back and pull my shirt off as well. Park's expression goes from surprised to awe. He leans back on his heels and runs his hands up my belly, to my ribs and on to my bra. I am not waiting for him to ask permission this time. I will not back out. I want this. I need this.

I wrap one hand around his neck and pull myself up, kissing his neck and tracing my tongue down to his collar bone. With my other hand, I reach around and unhook my bra, then pull it off and let it fall to the floor. Park moans when I kiss his neck again and then he slides both hands down my back and around my butt. He presses into me, our flesh colliding in ways that make me shudder.

"Off," I whisper as I tug on his jeans. He takes them off quickly, leaving on nothing but his boxers. I do the same with my jeans, but I let him help me pull them off.

"I love you so much," he says as he tosses my jeans to the floor.

I'm lying on my back in the middle of Park's bed while he needs at my feet, smiling. I'm exposed, vulnerable, and yet I don't feel any worry anymore. No anxiety about my body or fears that he won't like me for me. Even when he leans forward and the muscles in his arms flex, reminding me that he is so out of my league, I don't question his love for me, not even once.

Chills prickle over my skin when he slides his calloused palms up my thighs, up and up until his thumbs hook under the waistband of my panties. He kisses the flesh just below my belly button and a title wave of pleasure rolls through my body.

He looks upward with his lips still kissing me. Our eyes meet and I have to gasp for air because I hadn't been breathing. He trails kisses up my body, across my ribs and over my breast. I squirm with desire until his lips meet mine and his warm chest matches up with mine as he hovers over me. His hips press into mine and his need makes mine grows stronger.

Park's eyes search mine. "Are you ready?" he asks.

I slide my hands up his back, reveling in the power of love, the feel of his body next to mine. "Yes."

About the Author

Amy Sparling is the author of The Summer Unplugged Series, The Devin and Tobey Series, Deadbeat & other awesome books for younger teens. She also writes books for older teens under the pen name Cheyanne Young. She lives in Houston, Texas with her family and a super spoiled rotten puppy.

Amy loves getting messages from her readers and responds to every single one! Connect with her on one of the links below.

Connect with Amy online!

Website: www.AmySparling.com
Twitter: twitter.com/Amy_Sparling
Instagram: instagram.com/writeamysparling
Goodreads: www.goodreads.com/Amy_Sparling

Made in the USA
San Bernardino, CA
10 January 2019